Ladybird would like to thank Jane Swift for additional illustration work

Published by Ladybird Books Ltd
A Penguin Company
Penguin Books Ltd, 80 Strand, London WC2R 0RL, UK
Penguin Books Australia Ltd, Camberwell, Victoria, Australia
Penguin Books (NZ) Ltd, Cnr Airbourne and Rosedale Roads, Albany, Auckland, 1310, New Zealand

1 3 5 7 9 10 8 6 4 2

© LADYBIRD BOOKS MMV

Printed in Italy

Busy
Fire Station

written by Melanie Joyce
illustrated by Sue King

Ladybird

It's a very busy day at Busy
Fire Station.
Ding-a-ling-a-ling! the emergency
bell rings.

Fireman Fred and Fireman Jim
jump into their big red fire engine.
Don't they look smart in
their uniforms!

The fire engine whizzes off at top speed.
Nee-nar! Nee-nar! wails the siren.

There's a lot of traffic in
Busy Town.
But guess what?
It all moves out of the way!

At number 65 Fishpond Drive,
Grandma Lizzie is stuck up
a tree.
"What have we here?" asks
Fireman Fred, scratching
his head.

"How does a grandma get stuck up a tree?"

Fred gets the ladder and Jim
climbs up.
In no time at all Grandma Lizzie
is safe and sound.

Everyone claps and cheers.
Grandma gives Jim a great
big kiss. Ahhh!

Suddenly there's a noise.
Mr Sticks comes running.
He waves his arms.
"Fire! Fire!" he shouts.
It's lucky that Jim and Fred
are close by.

They're off like a shot.
But where's the fire?

In the back garden Jim and Fred roll out the water hose. It's ready to whoosh when suddenly… "STOP!" cries a voice. "There isn't a fire! It's the barbecue burning my sausages!"

Poor Mrs Bun, she nearly got soaked.
Good job nobody turned on the tap!

Just then there's a call on
the radio.
"Go to number 21 Plumtree
Drive," says the controller.

"Billy Boyle is stuck in the bath."
How could he get stuck in
the bath?
Fred and Jim rush to find out.

The fire engine whizzes off at top speed.
Nee-nar! Nee-nar! wails the siren.

There's even more traffic in
Busy Town.
But guess what?
It all moves out of the way!

At Plumtree Drive the bathroom is busy.
Billy's toe is stuck in a tap.
He's really worried.

"What if it never comes out?"
he groans.
"Don't worry," smiles Fireman Fred.
"We'll soon put things right."
And they do.

Jim and Fred use special tools.
They tap and turn and rub
on grease.

With a gentle pull, Billy's toe
pops out.
Everyone's happy. Especially Billy!

It's been a long day at
Busy Fire Station.
Fireman Fred is really tired.

"Don't worry," smiles Jim. "I've got just the thing. A mug of hot chocolate will put things right." And it does!